the CRiTTeR club

Liz at Marigold Lake

by Callie Barkley ❤ illustrated by Marsha Riti

LITTLE SIMON

New York   London   Toronto   Sydney   New Delhi

LITTLE SIMON

An imprint of Simon & Schuster Children's Publishing Division   1230 Avenue of the Americas, New York, New York 10020 Copyright © 2013 by Simon & Schuster, Inc. All rights reserved, including the right of reproduction in whole or in part in any form. LITTLE SIMON is a registered trademark of Simon & Schuster, Inc., and associated colophon is a trademark of Simon & Schuster, Inc. For information about special discounts for bulk purchases, please contact Simon & Schuster Special Sales at 1-866-506-1949 or business@simonandschuster.com. The Simon & Schuster Speakers Bureau can bring authors to your live event. For more information or to book an event contact the Simon & Schuster Speakers Bureau at 1-866-248-3049 or visit our website at www.simonspeakers.com. Initial interior sketches by Tina Kugler. Designed by Laura Roode.
Manufactured in the United States of America 0415 FFG
10 9 8 7 6 5 4 3 2
Library of Congress Cataloging-in-Publication Data Barkley, Callie. Liz at Marigold Lake / by Callie Barkley ; illustrated by Marsha Riti. — First edition. pages cm. — (The Critter Club ; #7) Summary: Liz is excited that her three best friends are visiting her family's cabin at Marigold Lake, but something seems to go wrong with every activity she planned. [1. Nature—Fiction. 2. Sleepovers—Fiction. 3. Best friends—Fiction. 4. Friendship—Fiction. 5. Clubs—Fiction.] I. Riti, Marsha, illustrator. II. Title.
PZ7.B250585Lh 2014 [Fic]—dc23 2013013011
ISBN 978-1-4424-9525-8 (pbk)
ISBN 978-1-4424-9526-5 (hc)
ISBN 978-1-4424-9527-2 (eBook)

Table of Contents

Sleepover at the Lake!

Squee-onk! Squee-onk! A loud, shrill sound woke Liz Jenkins. *My alarm clock sounds broken,* she thought, only half-awake.

Liz rolled over in bed and rubbed her eyes. No, it wasn't her alarm clock. It was a goose honking! Sunlight shone in through the window. Birds chirped outside. It was going to be a beautiful spring day at the cabin.

Liz threw off her flannel sheets and jumped out of bed. "Yes!" she cheered. "It's the perfect weather for the girls' visit!"

Liz's three best friends, Ellie, Marion, and Amy, were coming up to the Jenkins' lake cabin *today* for the three-day weekend. For years, they had heard all about it from Liz. She and her family had been coming to Marigold Lake since Liz was little. But this was the first time Liz had been able to invite her friends.

Liz hurried to change into her clothes. She had lots of things to get ready before the girls arrived. She

wanted their first visit to the lake to be perfect.

Out in the cabin's living room, Liz's mom, dad, and big brother, Stewart, were already up. Her dad was making breakfast. Her mom

was sweeping up pine needles from the floor. Stewart was setting the table.

"Oatmeal in ten minutes, Lizzie!" her dad said.

"Thanks, Dad," Liz replied. She was headed for the door. "I'll be back. I just need to do a few things."

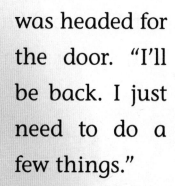

Outside, Liz took a deep breath. *Ahhhh.* Fresh air. She

smiled at the sight of the big, beautiful lake in the cabin's backyard.

Liz went into the storage shed. She dragged a folded-up tent to a flat area by the campfire pit. "Just the spot," Liz said out loud to herself. She would ask her mom or dad to help her set up the tent later. It

was definitely warm enough for the girls to sleep outside in it. Liz couldn't wait to surprise them!

Next, Liz hurried down to the boat dock. She took the tarp off the red canoe and made sure the life jackets were there. *We can paddle around the whole lake,* she thought.

Then, on her way back to the cabin, Liz picked up every long, thin stick she saw. *We're* definitely *roasting marshmallows over a campfire*, she decided. She left her pile of roasting sticks next to the campfire pit. Liz stopped to think. Canoeing, swimming, camping out, marshmallow-roasting, plus hiking on the nature path . . .

I hope we have time for everything! she thought excitedly.

Back inside the cabin, Liz joined

her family at the table. They had already served her oatmeal and yogurt—their usual super-healthy breakfast. Her dad passed her some berries to sprinkle on top while Liz told them about her preparations.

Liz's parents smiled. "Sounds like you've thought of everything," her mom said.

Then Stewart added, "But won't you guys just be painting your nails and stuff? Or whatever you do at your sleepovers?"

Liz rolled her eyes at her brother.

"*Actually*, my friends are so excited to have a wilderness weekend. I told them about all the animals up here—the rabbits, squirrels, deer, and foxes."

Liz and her friends were different in lots of ways, but they all shared one thing: a love of animals. Together they ran an animal shelter called The Critter Club in their town of Santa Vista. They helped all kinds of stray and hurt animals.

"You told them about *all* the animals we've seen?" Stewart asked. "Like the snakes? And the bear we saw that one time?"

Liz hadn't exactly mentioned *those*. Her friends weren't as excited as Liz was about unusual animals. Like the cool pet tarantula they took care of at The Critter Club over the summer. Ellie, Marion, and

Amy were glad Liz wanted to be in charge of it.

Liz shrugged and ate her oatmeal. *My friends will love the lake as much as I do!* she thought. *Or almost as much. Or at least they'll like it a lot.*

Welcome to the Wilderness!

Ellie's mom's van pulled up to the cabin just after lunchtime.

"Liz!" Ellie cried, jumping out of the back of the van. "Oh, we have missed you!"

Amy and Marion jumped out behind her. Marion giggled. "We just saw her *yesterday* at school," she reminded Ellie.

"I know!" said Ellie. "But so much has happened since then."

Liz and her family had driven to the lake the day before—on Friday afternoon. So Liz had missed the girls' after-school duties at The Critter Club.

"Don't worry, Liz," Marion said. "We'll get you all caught up."

The four girls huddled for a group hug. "I'm so glad you're here!" Liz told them. "Now the fun can begin!"

They said goodbye to Ellie's mom. Then Liz led her friends

down to the lake. They sat on the
boat dock. There the girls told Liz
the latest Critter Club news.

"First of all," said Amy, "our stray isn't a stray anymore."

Liz gasped. The girls had been taking care of a stray cat for a few weeks. "She's been adopted?" Liz asked.

"Even better," said Ellie. "Her owner called! He saw the ad you drew for the newspaper, Liz. Oh I brought a copy."

Liz's family didn't get the paper at their cabin, so she was excited to see her art in print.

Stray Cat Found!
Gray female with
white patches.
Sweet, gentle, very healthy
Can you give her a home?
Call The Critter Club!

"It was so sweet," said Marion. "The cat saw him and jumped right into his arms."

"Oh! And Grandma Sue stopped by yesterday," Ellie added.

Grandma Sue wasn't Ellie's grandmother. The girls just called her that. They had met her when they delivered a singing telegram to her from her grandchildren.

"She came with her new lovebird, Princess Two," Ellie went on. "Princess Two and Princess Boo are already best friends."

The girls had helped Grandma Sue when Princess Boo was acting

strangely. With the help of Amy's mom, a veterinarian, they figured out the bird wasn't sick—she was just lonely. That's why Grandma Sue had gotten a second bird.

"Oh, I'm sad I missed the chance to meet her," Liz said. But she shook off her disappointment. Her friends were here and they had the whole weekend ahead of them. "Let me show you guys around."

The other girls jumped up, ready to follow their tour guide.

Liz took them to the cabin. She pointed out the solar panels up on the roof. "All of our hot water is heated by the sun," Liz said.

She showed them the outdoor shower. "You can rinse off here after

a swim in the lake," she explained.

Liz took them inside. She showed them the shelves full of books and board games next to the fireplace.

Finally, Liz showed the girls her room.

"This is so great, Liz!" Ellie exclaimed.

"Yeah," said Amy. "No wonder you love it up here."

Marion was looking around Liz's room. "I *love* your room," she said.

"But there's only one bed in here. Where will *we* sleep?"

Liz's eyes lit up. "I'm glad you asked," she said. "Follow me."

Liz led the way back down

toward the lake. She stopped next to the campfire pit. "Ta-da!" she said, presenting the tent. Her dad had already set it up for them. "We can sleep here tonight. Won't that be the best?"

Liz looked at her friends' faces. Amy looked kind of excited. Ellie looked curious.

Marion looked worried. She glanced at Liz. She glanced at the tent. Then she glanced at Liz again. "You mean we're going to sleep . . . *outside?*" she said.

Chapter 3

Shivers and Jitters

"Last one to the floating platform is a rotten egg!" Liz shouted. She dove off the boat dock into the lake. She swam toward the platform. When she came up for air, she looked around.

Where were her friends?

Liz looked back at the boat dock. Marion was shivering, wrapped in

her towel. Ellie
and Amy were dipping
their feet in the water.

Ellie called out to Liz: "It's kind
of cold, isn't it?"

"Not really!" Liz called back.
"Just jump! It's great once you're in
the lake!"

But the girls didn't look so sure.
So Liz swam back to them.

Liz climbed out onto the boat dock. "I have an idea," she said to them. "Let's hold hands. On the count of three, we all jump in together. Okay?"

The girls looked at each other. One by one, they each nodded.

"One, two, three . . ."

They all jumped in with a *splash*!
When her head popped up, Amy
squealed loudly: "Eeeeeeek!"

"It's freeeeeeeeezing!" exclaimed
Ellie, half-laughing.

"Ohhmygosh, ohhmygosh," said
Marion, treading water.

"Keep swimming! Follow me!"

called Liz. "You'll warm up. I promise!"

The girls played Marco Polo and swimming tag. Soon they were having a blast. They floated on their backs and looked for pictures in the clouds. They talked while blowing bubbles in the water, seeing if each other could understand.

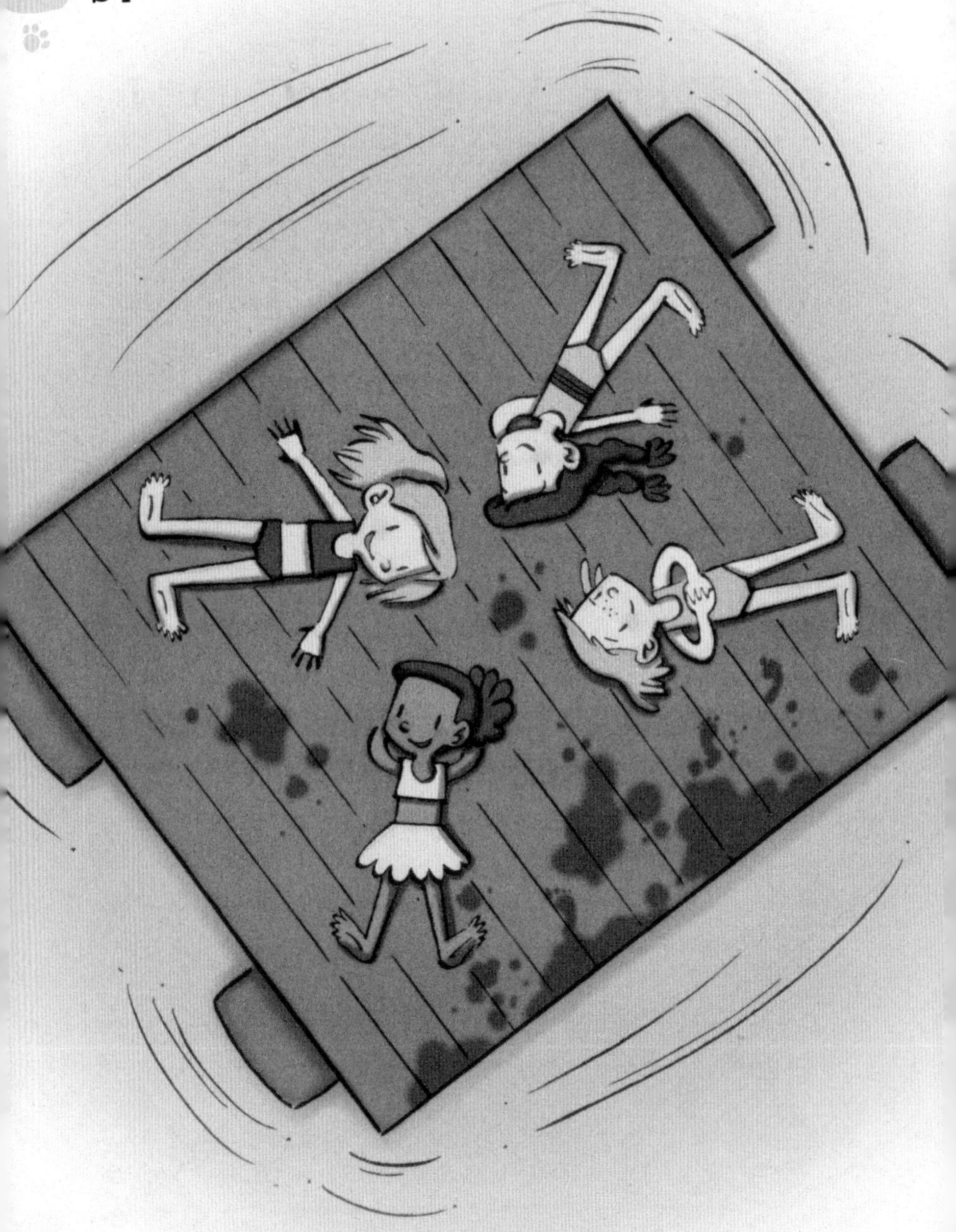

They were all laughing when they climbed onto the floating platform in the middle of the lake. The sun-warmed wooden planks felt nice as the girls stretched out to rest.

Then the breeze picked up. Before long, Marion, Ellie, and Amy were shivering.

"I think I'm r-r-ready to go in," Marion said. Her teeth chattered.

"Oh," said Liz, "okay." She had hoped they could spend a while doing silly jumps off the platform. But she didn't want her friends to be cold. So they swam back to shore.

Back on land, the girls changed into dry clothes. Liz's dad offered to take them on a nature walk.

"We can collect cool leaves," Liz suggested. "Then I'll show you how to make some fun leaf prints."

Ellie smiled. "Nature plus art," she said. "Sounds like Liz, all right!"

The girls laughed as they followed Liz's dad toward the nature trail. Stewart waved from the cabin porch. "Have fun! Watch out for snakes!" he called.

Ellie stopped in her tracks. "*Snakes?*" she said, her eyes wide with fear. "What snakes?"

A Very Short Walk

It took a while for Liz and her dad to reassure Ellie.

"We've never seen any *poisonous* snakes," Liz pointed out.

"That's right," said Mr. Jenkins. "And in *all* the years we've come to the lake, we've only seen a few snakes total."

Liz could tell Ellie wasn't so into

the nature walk anymore. But Ellie finally agreed to come along. "I want to walk in the middle of the group—not up front, not in the back," she said.

The nature trail went all the way around the lake. It was a walk that usually took Liz about an hour.

Just ten minutes down the trail,
Liz, Marion, and Amy already had
handfuls of leaves. Ellie was too
busy watching for snakes to look for
leaves.

"Here's my favorite so far," said Liz, holding up an oak leaf.

"I like this one!" said Amy.

"Oooh, birch!" said Liz. She knew a thing or two about the trees

around the lake.

Marion held one up. "How about this one?" she asked.

"Maple, for sure," Liz replied. "So pretty!"

Ellie sighed. "Oh,

I'm being ridiculous!" she said. "I want to find a special leaf too." She took one step off the trail, reaching down for a leaf. Her foot came down on the very end of a long stick. The other end popped up from underneath a pile of leaves.

Ellie jumped up and screamed. "Aaaaaaah! Snaaaaaaaake!" She took off, running back toward the cabin.

Liz's heart sank. Poor Ellie! It seemed the nature walk was over.

Chapter 5

Row, Row, Row Your Boat

Back at the cabin, Stewart was very sorry when he saw how upset Ellie was. After all, he was the one who had put the idea of snakes in her head. To make it up to the girls, he offered to take them on a canoe ride. "I'll row the row boat," Stewart said. "You guys ride in the canoe. We can tie the two together and I'll

47

tow you around the lake."

Ellie cheered up right away. "That sounds fun!" she said, beaming at Stewart. "But could I ride with *you*?"

Stewart shrugged. "If you want," he said.

The five of them put on life

jackets. Then Stewart tied a rope
line from the back of the row boat
to the front of the canoe.

Soon Stewart was rowing them
out into the middle of the lake. In

the canoe, Marion, Amy, and Liz lounged and relaxed.

"I could get used to this," Marion said.

"Me too," said Liz. "Stewart has never, *ever* rowed me around the lake before."

The late-afternoon sun was getting low in the sky. The water on the lake was still, except for the pools made by Stewart's oars. Liz sighed. It was a peaceful, happy, perfect moment.

Just then, on the far side of the

lake, a very large bird came splashing down to the water as it landed.

Amy gasped. "Wow!" she cried. "Is that a great blue heron?" She leaped to her feet, straining to see.

"Wait!" cried Liz. "Don't stand—"

It was too late. Amy teetered, then lost her balance. She fell out of the canoe, her foot catching the side. The whole canoe flipped, dumping Marion and Liz too.

When Liz came up from under the water, the first thing she heard

was Stewart laughing. But Liz didn't mind. She started laughing too. Liz had lost track of the number of times she and Stewart had tipped the canoe over the years.

Marion started giggling too. "Good thing I brought an extra pair of shoes!" she said.

"Are you guys okay?" Ellie called from the row boat. Liz could tell Ellie was trying not to laugh at her wet friends.

The only one who did not look amused was Amy. Liz recognized the familiar flush of pink on her cheeks.

Amy was completely embarrassed.

The Campout

Inside the cozy cabin, a warm fire crackled in the fireplace. Liz sat at the table, watching her family and friends chatting happily. Her parents had made them all a big dinner.

But Liz was feeling blue—and not very hungry. She loved grilled tofu and beet salad and roasted organic sweet potatoes. But did her mom have to make it this week-end? *Couldn't we have spaghetti, or something I know my friends like?* she thought.

Ellie was mostly pushing the tofu around on her plate. Marion hadn't touched the beets. Amy was chewing slowly and taking lots of sips of water.

After dinner, the girls settled into

the tent. Their four sleeping bags fit inside perfectly. Liz's mom found extra flashlights so each of them could have one. Then she zipped the tent flap closed.

"Good night, girls," she said through the nylon. "Don't stay up too late."

In the flashlight glow, the girls crawled into their sleeping bags.

"Marion," said Ellie, "did you bring your notebook?"

"Of course!" Marion replied, pulling it out of her backpack. Marion was super organized. She

loved making lists, so she always had paper and a pen.

"Great!" Ellie exclaimed. "We can play Two Truths and a Lie."

"Oh yeah," Amy said. "That game we played last weekend at our sleepover!"

The girls took turns hosting a sleepover nearly every Friday night, so they knew a lot of sleepover games. To play Two Truths and a Lie, each girl got a slip of paper. She wrote down two things about

herself that were true and one that was not. Then the others had to figure out which one was the lie.

Liz stared at her paper, thinking. Then she wrote:

I love grilled tofu.

I once swam all the way across the lake.

Then she added:

I am having a bad weekend.

The last one should have been a lie, but it was actually the truth. Liz knew Marion didn't even want to sleep out here. Poor Ellie was freaked out by the snake-stick. And Amy was still embarrassed about tipping the canoe. Plus the lake was too cold for them, and the food was too weird.

Liz sighed. She crossed out her last sentence and tried to think of a different one—one that really *was* a lie.

Chapter 7

Some Squeaky Guests

Everything looks a little brighter with the sun, Liz thought the next morning. That's what her mom always said. She unzipped the tent flap and peeked outside. It was a new day. Liz was ready to leave yesterday's troubles behind.

"Sleeping out here was so fun!" Amy said. They were walking up to

the cabin for breakfast.

"Yeah!" said Ellie. "Can we do it again tonight?"

Liz nodded. She noticed Marion wasn't saying anything, but she tried not to worry about it.

On the porch, they passed the leaf prints they had made the day before.

"They're dry," Liz announced.

"They look so good!" Marion said, holding hers up.

"They really do," Amy agreed.

"Liz," said Ellie, "you've made us all artists!"

Liz smiled a huge smile. The prints *had* turned out beautifully. More important, her friends had fun making them. Maybe Ellie's snake-stick scare had been worth it after all.

Inside, the girls found Liz's parents huddled over a cardboard box on the kitchen counter.

"Oh girls," Mrs. Jenkins said, "are we glad you're here!"

Liz and her friends looked at one another, puzzled. "What's going on?" Liz asked.

"Well," Mr. Jenkins explained, "last night we heard some noises."

Liz's mom nodded. "Little tiny squeaks. Coming from somewhere inside the cabin. And this morning, we found what was making them."

She nodded toward the box. The girls came over to look inside—and gasped.

"Awwwwww," Liz cooed.

"They're adorable!" cried Ellie.

Cuddled together on a kitchen towel at the bottom of the box were a bunch of tiny animals. They were covered in a light brown fuzz. They

had long, skinny, pink tails and rounded ears. Their eyes were shut tight.

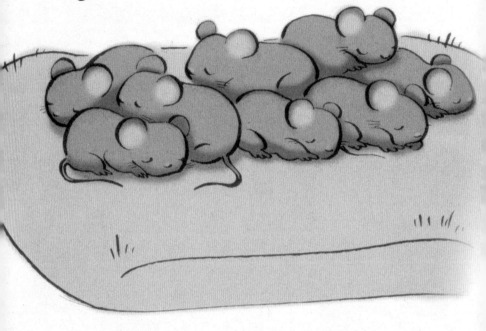

"Baby mice?" Amy asked.

Liz's dad nodded. "Yep! We found them in the back corner of

the pantry closet. There was a little nest too. But we can't find any sign of the mother."

"They looked so cold in there," Liz's mom added. "We thought they might be more comfortable in this box. There's a hot water bottle under the towel to keep them warm."

"What if the mother comes back?" Amy asked. "She won't be able to find them."

"Oh, no! She'll be so worried!" Ellie said dramatically.

The girls thought for a minute. Liz's eyes lit up. "I have an idea!" she cried.

Liz got some scissors from a kitchen drawer. Carefully, she cut out a mouse-size hole on one side of the cardboard box. "A door for Mama Mouse," she explained.

Then Liz carried the box to the

pantry closet. She laid it gently in the back corner. "Now they're snug and comfy, but if their mom comes back, she can find them."

Liz's friends and parents agreed: it was the perfect solution. Liz felt very proud!

"There's just one more thing," said Ellie. "What if the mother *doesn't* come back?"

Chapter 8

Critter Sitters

The girls knew one person who was sure to have some answers: Amy's mom, Dr. Melanie Purvis.

Amy used the cabin phone to call her mom back in Santa Vista. Marion sat next to her. She took notes in her notebook to help Amy remember everything her mom told them.

"So?" said Ellie the moment Amy hung up the phone. "What did your mom say?"

Amy sat down in front of the fireplace. The girls gathered around, eager to hear all the info.

"Mom thinks they're probably about two weeks old," Amy said.

"And what did she say about the mother mouse?" Liz asked.

"Well," said Amy, "here's the bad news: she said if it's been more than a couple of hours, the mother probably isn't coming back."

Liz, Marion, and Ellie looked

at one another, not knowing what they could do.

"But there's good news," Amy said. "We can take care of them. They'll need our help to eat for a few weeks."

Huge grins spread across the girls' faces.

"The Critter Club's work is never done!" Liz exclaimed.

Marion showed them her notes. She had made a list of supplies they needed to take care of the mice.

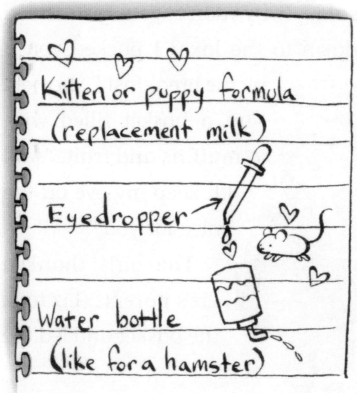

Kitten or puppy formula (replacement milk)

Eyedropper →

Water bottle (like for a hamster)

Liz's dad offered to go shopping. "There's a pet supply store in town," he said. "I'll run out and get what you need."

"In the meantime," Liz's mom said, "why don't you girls head down to the lake? I packed you a picnic breakfast." She held up a basket filled with muffins and fruit. "And I'll keep my eye on the mice for you."

The girls thanked Liz's parents. Liz took the basket and led the way down to the boat dock.

"So what should we do today?" Liz asked the girls as they nibbled on blueberry oat bran muffins. "There's a cool waterfall in the woods I could take you to."

Ellie frowned. "In the woods?" she asked. "How far into the woods?"

Liz sighed. *Oh right*, she thought. *Ellie's still nervous about the snakes.*

"Ah-CHOO!" Marion sneezed a huge sneeze.

"Bless you!" Liz, Ellie, and Amy said all together.

Marion sniffled. "Thank y—ah-CHOOOO!" She sneezed even louder and rubbed her eyes. "Uh-oh."

"What's the matter?" Liz asked.

"I just hope I'm not getting sick," Marion replied. "You know, from the chilly lake yesterday. I have a horse show next week that I do *not* want to miss. Maybe I'd better not swim today."

Marion rode her horse, Coco,

in all kinds of competitions. Sometimes they even won ribbons. Liz hated to think the trip to the lake had made Marion sick.

"And I guess I'd better stay out of the canoe," Amy said. "I don't want to dunk anyone again!" She said it with a half laugh. But Liz wondered if Amy still felt bad about the whole thing.

Liz turned her head away from the girls. She stared out at the lake. Her vision was getting blurry as her eyes filled with tears. She bit her lip, trying hard not to cry.

They hate it here, Liz thought.

Swimming is out. Canoeing is out. Hiking to the waterfall is out.

"Should we just take the baby mice and head back to Santa Vista today—a day early?" Liz asked them.

With the words out, she couldn't hold back the sobs anymore. Liz covered her face, turned, and ran off the boat dock.

Chapter 9

Friends to the Rescue

"Can we come up?" Ellie asked.

She, Marion, and Amy craned their necks, looking up at Liz. She was in a tree, about ten feet off the ground.

Liz nodded. "Yeah, sure." She sniffed. She wiped her eyes. She'd let it all out. Now she was feeling better— although maybe a little silly.

"Actually," Ellie called up, "can you come down?"

Liz looked down. The girls were having trouble climbing the tree. She couldn't help laughing through her sniffles. She had forgotten that

it took her one whole summer to figure out how to get up into that tree!

With a few quick moves, Liz was
back on the ground. "I'm sorry, you
guys," she said. "I just . . . I just had
all these ideas about how this weekend would be. I wanted you to have

a great time. I guess I didn't realize how much I wanted it."

Her friends moved in. They all wrapped their arms around Liz. Liz put her head on Ellie's shoulder.

"You don't have to say sorry for

being sad," Ellie said. "We're your best friends!"

"She's right," said Amy. "Friends should be honest about their feelings."

Marion nodded. "So we'll be honest," she said. "We *are* having a great time."

Liz looked up at them. "You are?" she asked. *"Really?"*

All three of them smiled and nodded. "Really!" they said together.

"But . . . but . . . ," Liz began.

She listed all the things that hadn't gone as planned: the snake-stick, the flipped canoe, the water that was too cold for them. "Nobody feels like swimming or canoeing," she added. "And now Marion might be getting sick."

Marion gave Liz a squeeze. "Oh, don't worry about that," she said. "I'll be fine. I just need to eat more of your mom's veggies, I guess."

"And yesterday was *so fun!*" said Amy. "We had a blast swimming— before we got chilly. Even canoe- ing was great." She giggled. "I can actually laugh about it now."

Ellie chimed in. "It makes a good story, that's for sure," she said. "And I know there's no reason to be afraid of a little snake. I'm in The Critter Club, after all!"

Ellie stood up straight and tall.

"So it's decided," she went on. "You're taking us to that waterfall. The one deep, deep in the woods. The deeper, the better!"

The girls laughed together.

"Aw, thanks, you guys," Liz said. "I feel so much better. You really are the best friends in the world."

"You too, Liz," said Marion. "And you're the world's best wilderness guide. So lead the way!"

Chapter 10

Campfire Chat

That night, around a glowing campfire, the girls roasted marshmallows with the sticks Liz had collected. Liz turned her stick slowly so her marshmallow cooked evenly all around.

Then, as they ate their treats, they talked about the day.

"My favorite part was the

waterfall, for sure," said Ellie. "I'm so glad I braved the evil snake-stick to see it."

"Well, my favorite was canoeing," Amy said. "I didn't even flip it *one time* today."

Marion put another marshmallow on her stick. "I think my favorite part of the day is still to come," she said. "You're not going to believe it: it's sleeping outside in the tent!"

"Really?" the girls said.

Marion nodded. "I've never done it before this weekend," she explained. "But I really like it. Being

out in the cool air, bundled up in a cozy warm sleeping bag, plus the sound of the crickets all around . . . It's the best!"

Liz gave a happy little clap. "Well, that does it," she said. "I think *this* is my favorite part." Hearing what her friends loved about the lake made her day. Then she had another thought. "This *and* taking care of the mice. They are just so cute. And they need us so much."

The mother mouse had not returned. So every few hours that day, the girls had fed the babies,

with the help of Liz's parents. They used the special milk Liz's dad bought at the pet supply store. They dripped drops

of it into the babies' tiny mouths.

"My mom says we have a tough decision ahead," Amy said. "After we bring them to The Critter Club, when the baby mice are bigger, they could be released back into the wild. They are wild animals, after all. Or we could try to find homes for them as pets."

Liz wasn't sure what the right thing to do was. "If we let them go, would they be okay?" she asked.

Amy shrugged. "It's hard to say," she said. "We would need to help them get ready. My mom says there's a special kind of mouse

house we could build for them. It would help them get used to living outside on their own."

Liz stared into the campfire. The flames jumped and danced. "It's funny," Liz said. "Tomorrow our wilderness weekend is over. But it turns out we'll be taking some of the wilderness home with us!"

It sounded like The Critter Club girls were going to have their hands full with the mice for a little while. Liz knew they'd figure out the right thing to do—together.

"So . . . , " Liz said slowly, "do you guys want to do another trip to the lake sometime?"

"*Yes!*" Ellie, Marion, and Amy all replied at the same time—and Liz knew they really meant it.

Read on for a sneak peek at
the next Critter Club book:

#8

Marion Strikes a Pose

Marion walked in the front door of Santa Vista Elementary School. In her head, she was going through her morning checklist: Homework folder? Check. Lunch box? Check. Sneakers for gym? Check.

Marion felt ready for the day.

She followed other kids into the auditorium for morning assembly, which they had every

Friday morning. She spotted an empty seat next to her three best friends, Amy, Liz, and Ellie.

Walking toward that row, Marion passed a group of fourth graders. "I love your skirt, Marion!" said a girl named Emily as Marion went by.

"Thanks!" Marion replied. She had spent a lot of time last night planning her outfit for today. She added one more item to her checklist. Cool outfit? Check!

Marion loved picking out her outfits for school. And for play dates and parties. And for riding her horse, Coco. For everything, really!

"Hi, Marion!" said Amy as she sat down. Farther down the row, Ellie and Liz waved.

"Attention, students!" The principal, Mrs. Young, spoke into the microphone at the front of the auditorium. All the kids quieted down. "I have some announcements. But first, we have a special guest. Her name is Hannah Eliot. She is the owner of The Closet, a store here in Santa Vista. Please welcome her." The students clapped.

Marion gasped. The Closet! It

was her absolute favorite clothing store.

Marion sat up straight in her seat as Hannah Eliot walked up to the microphone.

"Good morning, everyone," said Hannah. "Thank you, Mrs. Young, for letting me come today. I want to announce that we will be having a special fashion show at The Closet in a few weeks."

A fashion show, Marion thought. *How fun!*

"The purpose of the show is to raise money for a charity," said

Hannah. "It provides free clothing to children who need it, so it's a very good cause. We hope the fashion show will get lots of people to come shopping at our store that day. All the money we earn will go to the charity."

"What a great idea," whispered Marion. Amy gave a thumbs-up in agreement.

"But I need your help," Hannah went on. "Our store is a kids' clothing store. And I was thinking: Who knows best what kids like to wear? Kids! So I am looking for some young fashion designers."

Marion's eyes went wide. This was just getting better and better!

"The Closet is having a styling contest," Hannah explained. "To enter, you style an outfit—head to toe. I will pick one winning look from each grade. Those will be the outfits in our fashion show!"

Now Marion was so excited she could hardly sit still!

the CRITTER club

Join the club!

Visit CritterClubBooks.com for activities, excerpts, and the series trailer!